A NOTE TO PARENTS

When your children are ready to "step into reading," giving them the right books is as crucial as giving them the right food to eat. **Step into Reading Books** present exciting stories and information reinforced with lively, colorful illustrations that make learning to read fun, satisfying, and worthwhile. They are priced so that acquiring an entire library of them is affordable. And they are beginning readers with a difference—they're written on five levels.

Early Step into Reading Books are designed for brand-new readers, with large type and only one or two lines of very simple text per page. **Step 1 Books** feature the same easy-to-read type as the Early Step into Reading Books, but with more words per page. **Step 2 Books** are both longer and slightly more difficult, while **Step 3 Books** introduce readers to paragraphs and fully developed plot lines. **Step 4 Books** offer exciting nonfiction for the increasingly independent reader.

The grade levels assigned to the five steps—preschool through kindergarten for the Early Books, preschool through grade 1 for Step 1, grades 1 through 3 for Step 2, grades 2 through 3 for Step 3, and grades 2 through 4 for Step 4—are intended only as guides. Some children move through all five steps very rapidly; others climb the steps over a period of several years. Either way, these books will help your child "step into reading" in style!

Based on the TV series *Bear in the Big Blue House*™ created by Mitchell Kriegman.
Produced by The Jim Henson Company for Disney Channel.

Published in the United States by Random House, Inc., New York, and simultaneously in Canada
by Random House of Canada Limited, Toronto.

www.randomhouse.com/kids
www.henson.com
www.BearintheBigBlueHouse.com

Library of Congress Cataloging-in-Publication Data
Thorpe, Kiki.
Bear in the Big Blue House : Bear's shape book / by Kiki Thorpe ;
based on a teleplay by Jason Root ; illustrated by Joe Ewers.
p. cm. — (Step into reading. A step 1 book)
SUMMARY: Bear and his friends introduce the reader to a variety of shapes.
ISBN 0-375-80514-1 (trade) — ISBN 0-375-90514-6 (lib. bdg.)
[1. Shape—Fiction. 2. Bears—Fiction. 3. Stories in rhyme.]
I. Ewers, Joe, ill. II. Bear in the Big Blue House (Television program) III. Title. IV. Series: Step into
reading. Step 1 book. PZ8.3.T38Be 2000 [E]—dc21 99-29512

Printed in the United States of America February 2000 10 9 8 7 6 5 4 3 2 1

Bear's Shape Book

by Kiki Thorpe • Illustrated by Joe Ewers

based on a teleplay by Jason Root

A Step 1 Book

Random House 🏠 New York

Circle, triangle,
rectangle, square.
Come and find some
shapes with Bear!

"See the squares?
Take a look.

square

A box, a block,
a window, a book."

circle

"Balls and buttons, wheels and grapes— these things all have circle shapes."

"Triangle shapes are on a sail.

triangle

Rectangle shapes are in the mail."

rectangle

"A diamond shape
is on a kite.

diamond

Star shapes sparkle
late at night."

star

"I am not a circle
or a square.
What shape am I?
Please tell me, Bear."

"You are not a circle.
That is true.
The answer is
you are shaped like
YOU!"

"Just like a tree
or an ice cream cone,
you have a shape
of your very own."

"A pear has a pear shape,
and I have a Bear shape."

"Ray has
a sunny shape

Honey has
a runny shape."

"The Big Blue House has
a Big Blue House shape.
Tutter has a small blue
mouse shape."

"Pip has
a Pip shape.

Pop has
a Pop shape."

"A ship has
a ship shape.

A drip has
a drop shape."

"Here is a chance

to spot a bunch—

all kinds of shapes
are in our lunch!"

"Circles, squares,
triangles, too!
We love finding shapes…"

"Don't you?"